THE Chicken OF THE Family

Mary Amato

ILLUSTRATED BY **Delphine Durand**

  G. P. PUTNAM'S SONS

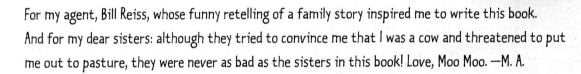

For my agent, Bill Reiss, whose funny retelling of a family story inspired me to write this book.
And for my dear sisters: although they tried to convince me that I was a cow and threatened to put
me out to pasture, they were never as bad as the sisters in this book! Love, Moo Moo. —M. A.

To Boubou and his family. —D. D.

G. P. PUTNAM'S SONS. A division of Penguin Young Readers Group. Published by The Penguin Group. Penguin Group (USA) Inc., 375 Hudson Street, New York, NY 10014, U.S.A. Penguin Group (Canada), 90 Eglinton Avenue East, Suite 700, Toronto, Ontario M4P 2Y3, Canada (a division of Pearson Penguin Canada Inc.). Penguin Books Ltd, 80 Strand, London WC2R 0RL, England. Penguin Ireland, 25 St. Stephen's Green, Dublin 2, Ireland (a division of Penguin Books Ltd.). Penguin Group (Australia), 250 Camberwell Road, Camberwell, Victoria 3124, Australia (a division of Pearson Australia Group Pty Ltd). Penguin Books India Pvt Ltd, 11 Community Centre, Panchsheel Park, New Delhi – 110 017, India. Penguin Group (NZ), 67 Apollo Drive, Rosedale, North Shore 0745, Auckland, New Zealand. (a division of Pearson New Zealand Ltd). Penguin Books (South Africa) (Pty) Ltd, 24 Sturdee Avenue, Rosebank, Johannesburg 2196, South Africa. Penguin Books Ltd, Registered Offices: 80 Strand, London WC2R 0RL, England.

Published simultaneously in Canada. Manufactured in China by South China Printing Co. Ltd. Design by Cecilia Yung and Marikka Tamura. Text set in Kosmik Flipper.

Library of Congress Cataloging-in-Publication Data

Amato, Mary. The chicken of the family / Mary Amato ; illustrated by Delphine Durand. p. cm. Summary: When her older sisters tease her into believing that she is actually a chicken, Henrietta runs off to a farm to be among her own kind. [1. Sisters—Fiction. 2. Chickens—Fiction.] I. Durand, Delphine, ill. II. Title. PZ7.A49165Ch 2008 [E]—dc22 2006003606

ISBN 978-0-399-24196-3 Special Markets ISBN 978-0-399-25268-6 Not for Resale

3 5 7 9 10 8 6 4 2

This Imagination Library edition is published by Penguin Group (USA), a Pearson company, exclusively for Dolly Parton's Imagination Library, a not-for-profit program designed to inspire a love of reading and learning, sponsored in part by The Dollywood Foundation. Penguin's trade editions of this work are available wherever books are sold.

H

enrietta had two older sisters
who loved to tease her.
   She hated it when they laughed at
her and made fun of her games.

One night, Henrietta was lying in bed,
trying to decide what to dream about, when . . .
"Boo!" Her sisters popped up beside her.
Henrietta screamed.

"We have a secret to tell you," said Kim, her bigger sister. "You're a chicken."

"Ha, ha," said Henrietta.

"It's true," Kim said sadly. "You really are a chicken. Mom got you from Barney's farm. Didn't she, Clare?"

Clare nodded.

"But I don't even look like a chicken," Henrietta argued.

"You do too," Kim said. "Your legs are yellow. And your toes are long."

Henrietta's legs were kind of yellow, and her toes were long.

"What about feathers?" she asked. "I don't have any feathers."

"Yes, you do," Kim said. "You grow feathers every night, and we have to pluck them out before you wake up. That's our job. It's why we get more allowance than you do. Right, Clare?"

Clare nodded.

Henrietta put her pillow over her head.

"I don't believe you."

Kim sighed. "What do you eat every morning
for breakfast, Henrietta?"

"Cereal."

"Aha!" Kim pulled away the pillow.
"That's what chickens eat! And
what do **we** eat every morning?"

"Eggs."

"Where do you think we get the eggs?"

"From the grocery store."

"Wrong," Kim said. "We get them from you."

"You do not!" Henrietta pulled her sheet over her head.

"Sweet dreams, Henrietta," Kim said.

"Sorry," Clare added.

Poor Henrietta tried to sleep, but she couldn't stop worrying.
What if they were telling the truth? She closed her eyes and chanted:

I am not a chicken.

I am not a chicken.

I am not a chicken.

The chant helped her fall asleep. When she
woke up, she jumped out of bed and looked
in the mirror. She wasn't a chicken. She was
a girl, a perfectly normal girl . . .

But there, in her bed, was an egg.
And on the floor by her bed were two
brown feathers. Her sisters were right.
She really was a chicken!

She crept down the stairs and peeked in the kitchen.
Her family was gathered around the breakfast table.

Kim was singing her "I love bacon" song, and Clare and her
parents were laughing and joining in. They sounded so . . . human.

Henrietta couldn't face them.
She had to find her real family,
so she slipped out the front door
and walked down the road to
Barney's farm.

She passed the barn and headed to
the meadow where there was a wooden
henhouse. A dozen chickens were out,
strutting in the long grass.

"It's me," Henrietta said. "I'm home."

A small brown chicken hopped from foot to foot and clucked.

Maybe she's my little sister, Henrietta thought. It would be nice to have a little sister for a change. Henrietta hopped and replied: "Bawk. Bawk. Bawk."

Another chicken flapped her wings.

Henrietta flapped.

The chickens strutted around, and Henrietta followed.

When the fattest hen ran over to a patch of dirt and flapped dirt all over herself, Henrietta did the same. After a while, the little brown hen started a game of tag.

Henrietta was "it" when Kim and Clare came on their bikes. Their faces were red from huffing and puffing.

"We've been looking for you everywhere. You've got to come home," Kim said. "Or we're in big trouble. Mom and Dad are mad at us because you ran away. Clare squealed and told them how we teased you about being a chicken."

Henrietta hopped from foot to foot.

"But I **am** a chicken."

"You aren't," Clare said. "We made that up."

"What about the egg in my bed and the feathers?"

"Don't be silly." Kim rolled her eyes. "We put those there to fool you."

Henrietta looked at the creatures calling themselves her sisters. "I don't believe you," she said.

"What a dumbhead!" Kim yelled. "You're not a chicken."

Henrietta turned to the brown hen. "You would never call me a dumbhead, would you?"

The hen stretched her neck and clucked. Henrietta sat next to her in the warm grass. "I **like** being a chicken. These chickens are nicer to me than you guys are."

"BUT YOU'RE NOT A CHICKEN," Kim screamed.

"This is a peaceful meadow," Henrietta said softly. "Please use a peaceful voice."

"Bawk, bawk," the white hen added.

Farmer Barney wandered up from his barn. "Hey, girls, what's all the squawking about?"

"Henrietta thinks she's a chicken," Clare explained.

Barney tipped his hat. "Chickens are the greatest. I wouldn't mind being a chicken myself."

Kim glared at him.

"Can I stay here with the other chickens?"
Henrietta asked Barney.

"Always got room for another free-ranger,"
he said, and headed back
to the barn.

Kim hissed, "You **want** to get us into trouble."

Henrietta shrugged. "I'm just a chicken. What do I know about trouble?"

Kim turned her bike around. "Come on, Clare, let's go."

Clare bit her nails. "Mom is going to be mad at us. I don't want to go home."

Kim rolled her eyes. "You are such a chicken, Clare."

Clare looked at Henrietta sitting in the grass. The sky was blue, the sun was warm, and the meadow smelled like hot apple pie. "Maybe I am a chicken," Clare said. "Can I be a chicken with you, Henrietta?"

"Always got room for another free-ranger," Henrietta replied.

Clare parked her bike and sat with Henrietta and the other chickens.

"I don't believe this!" Kim said, and then she rode away in a huff.

"So what do we do now?" Clare asked.

Henrietta grinned. "Let's play follow-the-leader."

Of course, Henrietta was the leader. She strutted and squawked and flapped her wings in a glorious, uproarious chicken dance, and everybody in the meadow joined in.

Oh, how wonderful to be a chicken after all.